# Chidi's Ad
# The Antelope

*For my family, friends and pupils who have been gems.*

Michaela Damasus Ritucci spent her early childhood in London and Nigeria. She now lives with her family in London and has written 30 children stories, some with her daughters. Her love of unconventional tales is both humorous and some times outrageous.

For more details visit the website
**www.akwocha.com**

# Chidi's Adventures
# The Antelope

First published in Great Britain in 2011
by Akwocha LTD.
P.O. Box 61261 Tottenham
London N17 1BW
England

Text© Michaela Damasus Ritucci  2011
Illustrations© Michaela Damasus Ritucci  2011

A catalogue record for this book is available from
the British Library.

Printed and bound in the UK
By MPG Books Group, Bodmin and King's Lynn

ISBN  978 1 908490 00 1

www.akwocha.com

# Chidi's Adventures
## The
## Antelope

# Michaela Damasus Ritucci

Granddad

Grandma

Uncle Dubi

Chidi

Obi

Tarik

Dengo-Tire

One hot, sunny Friday afternoon in Asaba, school finished, as it always did on a Friday, at 1.30pm.

Chidi and his father drove straight to Chidi's grandma Comfort's house in Ise. Ise was a small traditional village not far from Asaba. They were stuck in traffic so the journey, which on any other day would have taken only thirty minutes, took three hours. As they approached the front gate of his grandmother's house Chidi glanced at his watch. It was 4.30pm.

The car had barely come to a stop when Chidi opened the back door and jumped out, his backpack on his shoulders. He closed the door behind him and ran ahead, to open fully the gates of the compound. Dad gently glided the car into the compound. The welcoming sounds of withered leaves and dried twigs being crushed under the wheels of the car, made a soothing rustic sound.

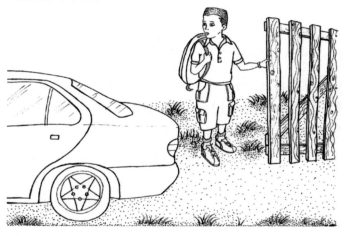

The car's engine was still running when Chidi rubbed his throat with his left hand and pushed the gate with the other. His throat felt dry for some reason. There was something not quite right about this feeling. He was sure that it was nothing to do with the air conditioning in the car. The air conditioning usually gave him an itchy throat, which he didn't have now. What he felt now was painless and strange, and his voice didn't sound normal.

"I must be coming down with something," he thought to himself.

There wasn't time for him to think any more about it. Dengo-Tier, gran's dog, was jumping all over him, wagging his tail.

Chidi knelt down, patted and hugged Dengo-Tier's head. He hugged him close to his chest while trying to adjust the straps of his backpack. When he got out of the car he had only put one of the straps over one shoulder. Now the weight on this shoulder was too much. He needed to spread the weight over both his shoulders to make his backpack lighter.

The realisation that his backpack seemed to now weigh a ton could only mean one thing: his mum had tampered with it. She must have repacked it with unnecessary items such as pyjamas and extra towels, he thought to himself. He only hoped that his computerised games and magazines were still in his bag. He now had to carry his backpack on both shoulders, being supported with straps. He hated carrying it this way, and voiced his thoughts aloud- , "Cos it's not cool and I look like a TOURIST!" Chidi turned to wave to his dad.

"I'll see you soon Son," shouted his dad, sticking his head out of the car window. Chidi's legs felt cramped as he stood still on one spot to stretch and yawn. As he stepped into his grandparents' compound, he began laughing silently and squealing with joy.

Gran's dog, Dengo-Tier, also known as Dengo, was Chidi's favourite of his grandparents' pets. His greetings really cheered Chidi up. It was said that Dengo was supposed to be a fierce guard dog, but at this very moment he was licking Chidi to death. Dengo was a huge, peculiar-looking golden-brown dog. He rarely barked, choosing instead to wag his long tail slowly if he was irritated. He was a slobbery dog, and dribbled when he was too hot. Growling was his way of protesting when he wasn't happy about something. He was however, fond of giving people pin falls and licking them, and he did this now to Chidi. To regain some kind of control, Chidi picked up a stick that was close by and threw it as far as he could. Dengo reluctantly went to fetch it, walking heavily, rather like an elephant.

Dengo-Tier thought that human beings were peculiar creatures who seemed to think that all dogs enjoyed fetching sticks. Well, he didn't. Oh no, not him. You see, he had grown tired of all these sorts of gimmicks, but even so he still felt obliged to participate in "fetch the stick" tricks. Dengo thought the saying that you can't teach an old dog a new trick was ludicrous. Why? He definitely wanted to learn new tricks. Fetching sticks seemed so outdated and so very boring. Dengo Tier was a unique dog. He understood many languages such as woof, miaow, meh

meh and moooo. Owl language, well that was hard, as it required certain pronunciations. Cricket and other insect languages were a little easier apart from bees. There was never time to respond verbally except the odd ouch while you ran for cover following a sting from one of the bees. He understood chicken language, Ibo, Yoruba, Hausa, English and a little Italian.

Chidi waved to his dad who was turning the car around to go back to Asaba. He stopped the car very close to the street, stuck his head out of the window and shouted to Chidi, "Greet Mama for me and tell her your mother and I will phone her this evening. Have a lovely time at the New Yam festival."

Still waving and feeling the weight of his backpack, Chidi acknowledged with a smile and nodded his head. He was still waving, when Dengo Tier returned with the stick. Another old saying sprang into Dengo's mind: *A dog's got to do what a dog's got to do*. And Dengo did just that. He turned his attention to what he most loved doing with Chidi. Chidi, knowing what was coming, had braced himself. As his father drove off, Chidi, looked at Dengo and exclaimed, as he had done so many times before, "Oh no! Don't you dare".

For a split second and "OOonly" for a split second, Dengo considered Chidi's command. But the pattern of this scene had been set. It was the end of the school term. He had to wait nearly six weeks for this moment. It was the day Dengo always looked forward to. He knew he was the lucky one unlike many other dogs in the village. Some dogs were happy to be guard dogs with no affections attached. Some were happy to be smothered by their owners with so much love that left them happy to retire peacefully at home. It still did not quench their thirst for living the wild life on occasions. He Dengo-Tier on the other hand, had the best of both worlds. He had gran and her family who gave him great love and chores he enjoyed doing. These chores comprised of rounding up the chickens, directing the goats where to clean up around the compound by eating up any left over litter and serving as a guard dog. He was also a working guide dog and enjoyed every moment of it. He also believed that all work, no play or fun call it whatever you like, makes Dengo an unhappy doggy. One member of gran's family who always made this play day a reality was Chidi.

He suddenly remembered that one of his chores had been to babysit Chidi years ago, when he was a small boy. Now Chidi had become an athletic kid, who enjoyed running and playing football. And he was currently training as a wrestler to take part in the village junior tournament. They had grown up together. How could Chidi begrudge him this moment?

Chidi and Dengo's relationship consisted of many things: competitiveness, friendship, equality, and most of all FUN, FUN, FUN! Dengo had trained with Chidi as he escorted him on brisk walks, they had rolled in mud together and Dengo had always been by Chidi's side. He was there while he rode his bike and when he was receiving instructions from gran. How could he possibly listen to him now? Obey him? NOW!

Dengo paused for a moment, but only for a moment. Then he made that familiar growling sound, "Ahrrrrrr ahrrrrrrr. Not now!".

The master dog relationship had to be put on hold. In fact, as far as Dengo was concerned, it had never really existed so he didn't feel he had to obey Chidi. Dengo, had always regarded his relationship with Chidi as equal. Chidi and he had always had that special buzz, a special relationship, and it was going to stay that way.

Dengo transmitted a telepathic signal to all the canines in the village, who for some strange reason, loved to line up in front of their homes to watch this great sportsmanship. It always occurred at the beginning of every holiday. It was popularly known as the **Freedom Run**, or **Woof Woof** in doggy language. Dengo stood upright on all four paws, with his tail up and ears now positioned to block out the noise of the traffic. His hind legs were ready to surge forward for the great race. Dengo began to chase dad's car. This was the moment he had been waiting for. He stayed close to the side of the road, occasionally running ahead of the vehicle.

As he passed the other dogs they began to bark harmoniously. Most of the dog owners knew that this barking and howling signalled the arrival of Comfort's boy. Some of the dogs were unable to contain their excitement; some fainted, some ran round in circles chasing their own tails, and some stayed rooted to one spot or stood on their back feet.

As the wind blew in Dengo's face, it made him look distorted and mangled. But that was fine! For Dengo, this was a real doggy-heaven treat. He paused occasionally to see if Chidi was keeping up. Sure enough, Chidi was, incredibly, doing just that.

"Come back, Dengo, before you get us both in trouble!" bellowed Chidi. Chasing after Dengo had left Chidi struggling to hold on to his backpack. He stopped for a while and gasped for air. This was a flawless performance that both Chidi and Dengo had perfected over the years. Increasing since Chidi began visiting his grandparents on his own. It was remarkable, that they both always managed to duck safely out of the way of the fast-moving vehicles.

Meanwhile, the traffic had slowed down for some reason. Some drivers who knew Chidi's family honked their horns to greet him and drove slowly past to ask how he was.

"When did you arrive?"

"Just a little while ago Auntie/Uncle/Sir/Sister/Brother/Chief/ Mr and Mrs," replied Chidi, greeting the questioners appropriately, according to the person he was talking to. Remarkably this was done well as he jumped over the puddles and potholes he was so familiar with while running after Dengo.

Drivers and bikers who were not familiar with his family made different comments:

"You de craze, Ohh!"
"Get yourself off the road!"
"You won die, foolish boy?!"
"No be me go kill you idiot!"
"Abo shere!" (Are you crazy?)
"Ewu!" (Goat!)
"This no be Olympics!"

Chidi's reply was always "Sorry Sir, Ma, Chief…"

Chidi was distracted as he caught sight of an important person nearby. Unable to stop running after Dengo, for the very first time as there is always a very first time, he knocked over a woman's basket of plantain that was resting on the pavement.

She was about to give him a clip around his head when she stopped. Her hands were still up in the air, just as the King known as Eze appeared. He was surrounded by a small entourage, but was still quite close to Chidi and Dengo. They had also caught sight of the king, and had both changed their pace from running to a subtle trot which slowed to a walk.

Chidi stopped to pay his respects to the king by bowing his head. The king was barely recognisable, as he was not wearing his regal clothing. Chidi however noticed that he wore the royal crest in the form of a necklace and his ring. He also wore jeans trousers, a white shirt, brown sandals and a baseball cap that had been made in Akwocha.

The king recognised him and asked, "Aren't you Comfort's grandchild?" "Yes, your Royal Highness," replied Chidi.

"Greet her for me," the king requested. Then smiling at Chidi, he asked "How is your wrestling coming on, my little one?"

"Fine, thank you Sir," replied Chidi as both he and Dengo froze in awe and respect.

The king's gaze suddenly turned to the lady standing near Chidi with a sorrowful look his head slightly bowed. Her basket of plantain still laid on the floor that Chidi and his accomplished had knocked over.

"Is there something wrong with your hand, madam?" he asked.

"No, my Eze" replied the woman.

The king picked up the basket and began to collect the plantain and return it to the basket and gestured to Chidi to do the same. This made the woman very happy. "What a lovely dog," remarked the king as he gave Dengo Tier a pat on the head. "How is your grandmother?" he asked Chidi when all the plantain had been returned to the basket.

"Fine thank you Your Highness," replied Chidi with a puzzled look, wondering how the king knew who he was.

As though reading Chidi's thoughts, the king leaned forward slightly so that he was at eye level with Chidi and whispered, "I did the same thing to your grandma when I was your age. Unfortunately I wasn't fast enough to avoid her and she clipped me at the back of my head."

The king turned to the lady selling the plantain and paid her for her trouble. He thanked her for her patience then he got into a car and was just about to be driven off when the car stopped "See you at the festival," he said to Chidi as the window began winding up.

Chidi and Dengo continued their chase, still thinking about what had just happened. Little did they know their performance, had been watched by passers by. It had created a heated debate in a bus that was nearby called the Danfoe. The opinions of the travellers were divided into two groups. Those from Ise were of one opinion, and travellers from Asaba were of a different opinion. The inhabitants of these towns were always in competition with one another, and Chidi and Dengo's antics were just another reason to disagree.

**Bang goes the unity**

The bus scene was a remarkable event. Chidi and Dengo Tier, had caused a heated debate. The subject focused on which village was better at raising children and why. Folks from the village of Ise, were convinced that their children were far better behaved than those from Asaba. Needless to say that folks from Asaba, thought the same about their own children.

*A lady from Asaba:* "I must say, I have never seen such an unruly child, running after a dog on the pavement like that! You wouldn't see that type of behaviour in Asaba," remarked the somewhat huge lady.

*A Man from Ise: replied* "That's because there's no room to run around in Asaba **that's why**!"
The man was clearly not too happy that his dear beloved village had been spoken about this way. He went on:

"In fact, Asaba has no land at all because you have littered the landscape with commercial buildings." The man's voice seemed to get louder and angrier as he pointed out of the window to illustrate his point, even though he was in Ise.

Folks who were from Ise jointly raised their voices to say **"We Agree"**, **"that's right yahhhhh"** with their arms waving above their heads.

*The reply from an Asaba folk was quick* "Is this what you call land?" his finger pointing out of the bus window. "This is just bush" one lady said. "And an unsophisticated one as well," cynically said by another elderly gentleman who was on his way back to Asaba.

"Look at all the children playing. At least they're breathing fresh air here in Ise. And you people from Asaba, only come to Ise to collect yam, plantain, gari and casava. You need what we provide here."

The arguments continued until the driver had enough. He shouted, "No politics here please, otherwise you get off the bus at once. You hear me so?"

The debate quietened down and the occupants of the bus murmured under their breath, each quietly insulting the inhabitants of the other village and calling them names. After a while silence fell inside the bus, as they drove past Chidi and Dengo who were completely unaware that they had started such an exchange.

After a while, dad and the car could no longer be seen. Dengo walked back to Chidi very slowly, deliberately keeping his head down towards the floor. He was determined to avoid eye contact with Chidi. He knew he was furious with him and wanted to say something once he had caught his breath. As he always did, Chidi wagged his finger at Dengo and scolded him. "One of these days I will get rid of you! Look at you! You look like a big dog."

"Huhhhh Dengo thought to himself "I am a big dog! Look at you, you look like a boy" he smugly thought to himself. "You always say that you'll get rid of me every time. You know you won't" still thinking to himself.

They both stopped to stare at each other for a while, before heading off to gran's place without speaking to each other.

Chidi was about to speak again when his throat suddenly felt strange again. He put his hand up to rub it. What was going on? he thought to himself. Briefly forgetting what had just transpired, he and Dengo turned to begin their walk back to gran's house, in silence.

## The welcome at grandmother's house

Chidi pushed open the large gate, and walked into the compound with Dengo. He was listening to some music through his earplugs, while enjoying the familiar sights and smells all around him. He took out his mobile phone, switched it to silent mode, and placed it back into his pocket.

His grandparents' house always never seized to amaze him, even though he always stayed here during the holidays, for as long as he could remember. The first thing any visitor would notice was the path leading up to the house, or rather the houses.

The path was lined with an assortment of fruit-bearing trees, such as mangos, paw-paws and fruits called udalahs. Some of the fruits had fallen to the ground, and you could see the freshly cut stems where some of the fruit had been picked. The red soil was slightly hot under Chidi's feet, even with his sandals on. Some of the trees provided a welcome area of shade from the sun. Chidi was enjoying one of such shades, when a growl from Dengo attracted his attention. A bright orange lizard landed on the ground right in front of him. It made eye contact with him for a very brief moment, and nodded its head.

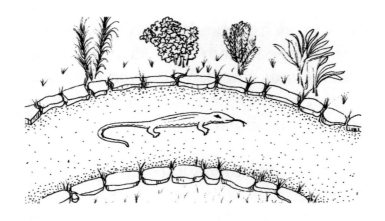

"Hello little fellow," said Chidi, as he carefully put down his bag. He bent down to get a closer look at the lizard. He managed to stroke its head, then Dengo growled again, sending the lizard scuttling off into the bush.

"You again!" sighed Chidi. He turned to stare at Dengo. Then he closed his eyes and slowly stood up clenching his fists. He took a deep breath, gave Dengo a very stern stare and said in a low voice, "You'd better stay out of my way," then carried on walking.

After a short walk, the buildings came into view. Only a few yards to go, until he was at his grandparents' home. As he emerged from the shade of the trees, Chidi shielded his eyes from the glaring sun. Dengo had overtaken him and walked on ahead.

Gran's accommodation was split into two parts. The modern part was a large, spacious bungalow that had been painted white. This had a veranda, with a large porch that was designed to serve as a sitting room. The inside was sheltered from prying eyes by round-holed bricks that grandma hated. They made her feel as though she was caged in. Chidi's mother and her siblings had insisted on building this part of the house, despite grandma's objections. They had always wanted to build a modern home for their parents, and wouldn't take **no** for an answer.

A long corridor separated this modern part of the house from the traditional part. The traditional part of the house was made from red bricks and was painted with earth-red paint. It had large windows with wooden shutters. The corridor and the entrance into the main traditional house were adorned with traditional paintings and decorations. Grandma loved this traditional side of the house, and spent all of her time here rather than in the modern part.

Nodding his head to the music playing from his mobile phone, Chidi was fast approaching the main house. He suddenly stopped briefly to marvel at the scenery. He always loved walking along the path. It made him feel he was at one with nature.

His mobile phone suddenly began to ring. He brought it out of his back pocket and checked to see what number was calling him. It was a well-known number. He hesitated momentarily.

His trigger-happy thumb that seemed to have a mind of its own **betrayed him.** It pressed the green receive button, and in a quick instance he began to wish the transmission would break up. However hard he wished, it never happened. He spoke to his mum.

"Hi mum. I'm almost at grandma's house." He paused to listen to what his mother was saying to him and froze with shock. His mum was telling him that his sister Neka was going to clean up his room while he was away.

"Please keep Neka away from my room," he pleaded. But his mum didn't listen. As usual she continued talking to him about a number of things, or rather reminding him of the rules which were clearly of no interest to Chidi. He was relieved when the call finished and he switched his phone back to silent mode. Chidi muttered under his breath, repeating or rather mimicking what his mother had said to him on the phone:

"Don't go in the stream. Wear long trousers in the evenings. Don't cut firewood. Use the tap water and not the well water.' Honestly, mum, that's the least of my problems. Nothing can be worse than Neka in my room, going through my things, invading my privacy, violating my human rights…" groaned Chidi.

He soon forgot his troubles when he arrived at his grandma's house.

Loud shouts and the laughter of his grandparents and their visitors reached his ears.

Chidi was in awe at what he was witnessing. What was it that mum and her siblings had wanted for his grandparents? Oh yeah, they wanted them to live 'a tranquil lifestyle', to live in a place where the cool air and the sound of birds singing would be their companions for the rest of their lives.

"Ha! Wishful thinking mum" Chidi said to himself with a chuckle. With all the parties his grandparents hosted that was never going to happen. There were a lot of friends and relatives who always seemed to be at the house. gran's place served as a social club. Besides his grandmother was the local Midwife who delivered babies. She was also the vet and the lady in charge of lady affairs. His grandparents were still defying what their children thought would be best for them. It was almost as if they had reversed roles with his mum and some of her brothers and sister. It was as though they were the children disobeying their parents' wishes.

Chidi was greeted by a stream of guests. Mostly relatives, there were women at the back of the house, children at the side of the house and men playing Eyo or cards with granddad. Eyo was a game played with seeds, small stones or beads had to be spread evenly into a container, a little like an egg-box. The fresh smell of pepper soup was inviting too. Chidi turned to get a bit of support from Dengo Tier, stretching out his hand to stroke him, only to find that he had stayed outside like a guard dog. Dengo would not dare to mess with Gran.

An old slim looking man was seated on the veranda with a pipe in his hand. He was tall and fair; most people called him Oyibo ('white man'). Chidi was very proud of his granddad and watched him for a moment, as he sat on the remnants of a seat from the train he had once driven. He was unable to get close enough to hug him though. Because he was intercepted by numerous uncles, who grabbed and hugged him. Some lifted him up in the air above their shoulders.

Chidi's granddad was equally proud of him and he reminded everyone that Chidi was his grandson. He spoke fondly of his daughter, Chidi's mother, and now reversed the role he had played when she had wanted to wed Chidi's dad.

"I knew the marriage would last and be successful," he said winking at his grandson, knowing full well he wasn't being completely truthful.
"Huh!" Chidi muttered quietly, grinning to himsef. That's not what he had heard. He recalled grandma telling him that his grandfather had objected to the marriage and had predicted that it wouldn't last. Grandma, on the other hand, had agreed to it.

Chidi was still being hugged by various relatives. Before he could object, his grand auntie, Granddad's sister planted a wet kiss on his cheek.

As if that weren't enough, Chidi almost suffocated. She had pressed his head close to her almost bare chest, as she only wore a loose wrap.

"Onowu wam, when last did you eat?" as she sort of shouted at him. Holding his arm up like a puppet, she began using her fingers, to measure how much fat he had on his arm.

Before he had time to answer or object, Chidi was given a plate of cola nuts by one of the young men. He was urged to join the other boys as they served the blessed cola nuts to the elders. It was the job of the youngest people at a gathering to serve the elders in this way. In return, the young servers were given some to taste. Chidi never ate any though, as cola nuts were extremely bitter. Instead he gave his share to one of his uncle nicknamed **Uncle Cola Nut**.

Such was the greeting Chidi received from his mother's relatives, that it overwhelmed him, every time he visited. Yes, this was Chidi's grandma Comfort's place. It was the most welcoming place on earth, where adventures were always just around the corner. One such adventure was always the New Year festival, also known as the New Yam celebration. He loved to attend the famous hunt which always started here at his grandparents' home. It had no modern finesse, no 'how do you do? No invitation was needed. People simply sat in any available space, on the steps, on fences, car bonnets, beneath trees, and became one with the crowd.

Chidi stepped back a little to look at the gathering. Without a doubt he knew that he was a part of this village and that this was his home. He felt a firm hand on his shoulder. Chidi recognised the touch and turned around to greet his favourite uncle. "Ah, Onuwu [Good day] uncle Dubie!" exclaimed Chidi, delighted to see his uncle. He was lifted high onto his uncle's shoulder, shrieking with great delight, before being gently lowered to the floor.

Chidi turned the volume of his music player down. He could still hear and participate in what was going on around him while it was playing. But he wanted to give his uncle his full attention. He pulled the earphone from his right ear, and threw himself again at his mother's little brother. He could still hear his favourite band, a group called Super Duck, playing his favourite song in his left ear. It was a blend of western dance and African music that sounded great on his phone.

Chidi loved his uncle very much. They had a lot in common. They shared the same taste in music, he was cool, and had an English accent. They also both loved wearing jeans and trainers, and playing the guitar and African drums.

"Onuwu, my little nephew," replied uncle Dubie, lifting Chidi off the floor.

"My, you have grown. You're almost as tall as me!" he exclaimed loudly in the deep voice that Chidi knew and loved.

"How are my cousins and when did you arrive from England?" Chidi asked excitedly.

"Your cousins are well, thank you, and I arrived three days ago. Have you come to join us for the New Year celebrations?" enquired uncle Dubie.

"Yes, I can't wait!" answered Chidi, but then his attention shifted to a girl called Amina. Chidi had known her since they were small children. She had blossomed into a lovely young girl. She was very clever, a talented dancer and horse rider.

Uncle Dubie chuckled realising that he had lost his nephew's attention. He was no longer interested in the little chat they were having. "I'll see you later," he whispered with a grin. He paused and watched his nephew turn to go and talk to Amina and her brother Tarik. He suddenly realised that his nephew was growing into a fine young man.

Amina's parents worked in the village as horse rearers. Chidi thought that she was so lovely. Tarik was one of his best friends. The family came from the northern part of Nigeria. They spoke the Hausa language, which his grandparents and mother spoke fluently. He called over to them, "Sanu!"

They replied "Sanu!"
"How is your sister?" Amina asked.

"Fine, thank you," Chidi replied.

He was just about to start a conversation, but was interrupted by his phone, silently vibrating in his back pocket. Much as he wished to, he couldn't ignore it.

"Excuse me a moment," he stuttered as he walked over to a nearby log to answer it. He was too late. He had just missed his dad's call. He didn't want to call back, not just yet, but then he remembered that he needed to speak to his dad as soon as he possibly could. His well-being depended on it.

Waving to Amina who was by now speaking to another childhood friend, Chidi sat down on the huge log. He had to tell his dad, to keep his mother and sister out off his bedroom, he called it his den. It was his sanctuary. He'd done everything he could think of to make his room uninhabitable: a fresh supply of smelly socks that were not put away, trainers that let off intoxicating fumes, leftover food such as towo. One of his favourite meals made from rice, mostly eaten in the northern part of Nigeria. He would often eat this when he visited Tarik and his family and pizza and other half-eaten food and, last but not least, dirty clothes strewn over the floor.

However hard Chidi tried, his sister Neka and his mum couldn't stay away from his room for any longer than a few days. Their craving for doing good to all mankind, always got the better of them. And it always seemed to happen after they had been to Mass, on a Sunday. His only hope was to persuade dad to divert their attention to something else. He began muttering to himself again, working out what he might do.

"Today is Friday. That means I have less than 48 hours left before they go to worship. Goodness knows what sermons they listen to at Mass."

Chidi broke out in a sweat. His self-proclaimed liberty and desire to live his life the way he wanted was about to be intruded upon. It was not his fault that the rest of the house was too clean and unable to sustain any other life forms. He sat on the log and texted his dad to call him back as he didn't have much credit left on his phone. According to Chidi's calculations, the celebrations here in Ise would be over by 10 o'clock on Sunday morning. That would give him thirty minutes to get back to his precious den at home. Who was he kidding? He would never make it home in thirty minutes. It would take him almost an hour to get back to Asaba. No make that an hour and a half but hopefully not 4, as the list of hours could be endless. The ritual of saying goodbye at Ise was astonishing. He had to say goodbye to his uncles, great-uncles, aunts and great-aunts, as well as all the other relatives. In-fact, he nearly had to say goodbye to practically the whole village. Then the relatives would give him fresh food to take home, food such as gari, plantain, onions and herbs. Oh yeah, and then there would be the prayers and the blessings that would be said over him before he set on his way. **YHAP!** It's not easy to be an African. The funny thing was that he didn't even know who half the people were, that gave him goodbye hugs and kisses.

His thoughts returned to how his mum and Neka would embark on their mission of redemption.

"The Sunday service ends at about 1.30pm and it will take them between 45 minutes and an hour to get home. I should be there by 3 o'clock..." His thoughts were interrupted by Dad returning his call.

Chidi tried to explain this to his father how important it was to keep Mum and

Neka out of his room, but his father had no clue what to do. He was hesitant to stall his wife and daughter, simply because he didn't know how. He just wanted a peaceful weekend. Chidi realised he had to give instructions to his dad, on how best to stall both mother and daughter.

**Chidi's instructions**
"Take note, dad. This is what you need to do." Chidi lifted his thumb in the air to start counting the instructions he was about give his dad.

"First, when mum comes back from church, she'll spend ten minutes sitting in the porch with her feet up. She'll want a run-down of everything that's happened while she was away from home for just two hours. Give her a glass of water, she'll take her time and drink it slowly, while she listens to everything you tell her. She'll take her shoes off and her headgear will be on her lap. This is where you need to ask her how the service was. She'll take at least ten to fifteen minutes to tell you. Be careful not to ask too many questions. Let her do the talking, she loves that.

"After that, she'll go into her room to put her clothes away. She'll fold them all and place them slowly and carefully into the trunk. She'll take another few minutes to remove her jewellery and admire it before she puts it away. Comment on some of it and encourage her to tell you when and where she got it. Stall her by admiring her jewellery, but don't commit to buying more for her!

"Then you'll all eat a meal. Get mum to rest for half an hour after that, then call Neka and ask her to recite the seven times table".

"Why?" asked dad, "and who'll bring you back.

"Neka hasn't mastered the seven times table yet. If my calculation is right it'll take her six hours to learn it. You know she's a sucker for perfection."

"What is a sucker?" enquired dad.

Chidi had forgotten that his dad hadn't quite mastered the understanding and use of modern slang words. Rather than try to explain the term "sucker" he rephrased it.

"Dad, what I'm trying to say is that Neka aims for perfection that's all," replied Chidi. He continued with his instructions. "Dad, try to give mum a task. Tell her you want a celebration cake and some bread. That should keep her busy!" Chidi laughed. "Uncle will Will bring me back."

The only response from his dad after the outburst of laughter was "Hmm."
Chidi sensed that his father was chickening out. His attempt to use gentle persuasion didn't seem to be working at all. There was no other option, other than to upgrade his tactics from gentle persuasion to 'you don't have a choice'. And it went like this:

"Oh yeah, dad, just remember that if you let Mum near my room, she'll find your box of collectable stamps, coins and vintage car magazines you keep in there".

There was a pause at the other end of the phone. Chidi heard his father's breathing become heavier. He continued. "And remember, there's also the ticket to the World Cup that you, me and granddad will need to get us into the stadium! I'm still working on an airtight alibi for us missing the big day for mum. You know, so mum will understand why we have to miss her birthday party, for her big Four O."Chidi knew this wouldn't fail. He waited for the words his father always uttered when he was in despair.

"Okoko," followed by a sigh "Huuuh Huuuh. "Please tell me again, my son, what I need to do. I hope you don't mind?"

"No, dad. I don't mind repeating what I've just said. We all have to stick together. Don't you agree?"

"I certainly do agree, Son," his dad responded. Chidi went through the details again, and dad really listened this time.

After they had confirmed all the details, Chidi smiled to himself. "I knew he'd see it my way in the end," he said to himself as he walked away from the log.

Chidi made his way back to the traditional part of his grandparents' buildings, to the main house in which they lived. He carefully placed his mobile phone in his pocket, and beckoned Dengo Tier to come along with him. He went round the back of the house to avoid being pulled around by the houseguests again. People were arriving all the time. Relatives were everywhere. He remembered that he had left Amina under a palm tree, but when he turned to look, she had gone.

Dengo Tier hesitated briefly when they got to the back of the house. A long time ago, Chidi's mother had banned him from using this entrance. Her fierce stare had left a long-lasting reminder in his memory. He was instead supposed to use the side entrance so he wouldn't get muddy footprints in the house. But Chidi needed him to come in this way with him. He grabbed him gently around his belly and pushed him inside. "Mum's not here, my friend, and grandma won't mind. Anyway, what do you have to worry about? You only see mum occasionally. Spare a thought for me I have to live with her and my sister," moaned Chidi to Dengo.

The thought made Dengo shudder as well so it seemed.

Chidi caught a brief glimpse of his grandmother at the back of the house. He climbed up the steps of the porch, pausing to wipe his feet on the mat. She was a tall, average sized, dark-skinned woman with long black hair.

"Onuwu Enyi Mama," said Chidi as he wandered where she was. Using the traditional local greeting reserved for highly respected citizens. "Sorry I am late." He put his hand to his throat again. It still felt strange.

Chidi threw his school bag on the floor, unbuttoned his shirt and kicked off his sandals. He was relieved to finally come into the cool part of the traditional house of his grandparents. He needed it after being cooped up in the car on such a hot day. Very few visitors were allowed into this part of the house. Granddad and uncle would see the guests off before too long. Right now, Chidi's main intention was to catch up with some much-needed sleep, on his gran's bed away from the guests.

Chidi stretched out on grandma Comfort's bed. It was so comfortable. Dengo Tier meanwhile positioned himself at the door just like a guard dog. Grandma wrapped her grandson in a red and white Akwocha. A cotton fabric woven by the locals, the fabric is used for special occasions such as weddings and left him to sleep. He didn't stir until early the next morning.

Chicken Dawn was the family's alarm clock. This morning as always, he crowed at the crack of dawn in his loud voice.

Chidi woke up excited that this was the day he would be going to the Town Square, to take part in the opening ceremony of the New Yam also known as New Year celebrations. The celebrations as always, was opened by the king. It would be attended by nearly everyone in the whole town, before they went off to the traditional antelope hunt.

Chidi wandered through the sitting area of the old house. The furniture in this part of the house was made from carved wood with beautiful sculpted figures. Gran had a gramophone as she loved to play her vinyl records. A large portrait of Gran, dressed in her warrior's clothes was mounted on the wall. She held an ISAKA, a shaker-type of instrument and an ekupe a traditional handmade fan. This signified that she was a Chief, rather like a Lord or a Lady. Chidi walked through to the back of the house. It was still very early. Grandma was standing nearby as he arrived outside. He greeted her in the traditional way, by bending forward slightly and saying, "Mama Enyi." Gran picked up her ekupe and placed it on Chidi's back as an acknowledgement of his greeting.

"Mama, why don't you have an alarm clock to wake me up?" asked Chidi. "What do you want an alarm clock for when Dawn the chicken, does the job for you as nature intended?" Grandma replied in surprise.

Although he didn't like being woken up that way, Chidi could see the point of what his grandma was saying, so he decided not to say any more. Instead he started to look for his toothpaste and toothbrush. "Oh no," he said to himself, "I've forgotten to bring my toothbrush and toothpaste. Have you got a spare toothbrush and some toothpaste Mama? I've forgotten mine."

"No," said his grandmother. "Use the chewing stick."

Chidi groaned inwardly. Not the chewing stick! "Where is it?" he asked.

"It's in the cupboard," she replied.

Chidi took the chewing stick from the cupboard and began to chew it. It was awfully hard to use. It was bitter and hard. He needed to chew it into a soft pulp to clean his teeth, and it took ages to do that. Chidi knew that his grandma loved nothing more than to use the chewing stick to clean her teeth she couldn't stand the taste of toothpaste. Chidi went outside to wash his face. It was not uncommon to see a traditional Nigerian home having an outdoor bathroom. Families washed outside designated areas using water from the wells. Chidi's grandparent's traditional home was no exception.

Chidi enjoyed using the outdoor washroom than the indoor one. The chewing stick was finally beginning to change into a pulp. At intervals he took sips of water to rinse out his mouth. He shuddered as he did this because of the bitter taste the chewing stick left in his mouth.

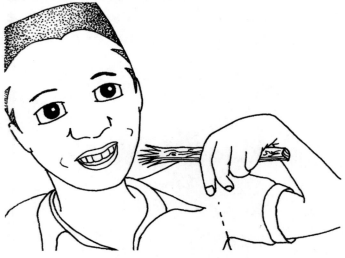

With his face washed and his teeth now clean, Chidi threw the chewing stick in the bin, lifted his head and looked around him. The bitter taste was soon forgotten as he was suddenly now wide awake, and transported into another world. He had come to cherish this world so much and he wished he could live here for ever. It was the fresh, early-morning mist and the smell of the red, damp soil that he loved so much. It invigorated his senses and awakened his body in a way that the town could never do.

Chidi looked around him. He could see a grasshopper with its green wings, its long, slender, shell-like body and its antennae sticking out of the top of its head. A spider's web had been carefully spun between the twigs of a nearby tree. Pearly drops of water hung from it, and the spider balanced lazily on it. At the corner of his eye he saw Okookoo the hen, perched on a basket, in the hen house laying eggs. Ewu, the goat chewing on the leftover food he had missed the previous day.

Chidi removed his slippers, and began to move his left foot from side to side. It made a semicircle in the sand. He lifted his right foot to see the print that was embedded in the sand. Closing his eyes he allowed his mind to become completely blank as he drifted into deep meditative thoughts. Absolutely not thinking of anything at all, he felt at peace. The moment was truly divine, a wonderful way to escape the busyness of the town life he usually lived in Asaba. This moment lasted for a few minutes before he awoke.

Chidi went to the ete to get a drink of water. In addition to having a modern fridge, grandma had a traditional ete. This was made out of red clay and looked like a giant jug. It was always filled with water to drink and it kept it incredibly cool. Chidi marvelled at this simple traditional invention, with its designs and vibrant colours that represented the culture of Ise. The ete kept the water cool, no matter how hot it was in the day, and gave the water a lovely, distinctive earthy taste.

Gran favoured the traditional ways of doing things. Food was always dried in the sun on a flat stone slab so it would last longer. She also had a red clay oven that used firewood and sometimes kerosene. Her cooking pots were made out of clay, and the family's water for drinking and cooking came from the well at the back of the house.

Grandma was sitting on a stool, cleaning her stainless steel pots and pans with sand. Chidi watched her for a while before asking her why she did it this way.

"The earth does many things for us, my child," she replied. "The sand is like a natural soap. Natural ingredients are so much better than modern chemicals or work alongside them. The sand cleanses the pots and removes germs. I am preparing for the New Year celebrations and traditionally this means we must use all that the earth has for us."

Chidi was fascinated by this information and was determined to remember it so he could bring it up in his chemistry lessons at school.

"Mama, will the hunting celebration soon begin?" Chidi beaming a smile, became excited and jumped up and down, clenching his fists. "I finally have the chance to capture an antelope and become a man," he shouted. He turned to his grandma and asked "Is it really true that if I do this I'll become a man?" Chidi failed to see the unhappiness he had caused as his grandma suddenly become silent. All he could think of, was the chance of proving to everyone that he had come of age. Now he was no longer afraid of the forest. He could work in a team and above all he wanted his name to be known in the village. It was especially important now he was turning twelve, a significant age.

"A man?" shouted grandma looking at Chidi sternly. Grandma was firmly against hunting. She was against animals being hurt for no reason and strongly believed that all living things should have the right to live. She stood up straight with her arms akimbo and said firmly, "You think capturing an animal that has been injured makes you a man?" She softened a little and continued, "No, my son. A great man is one who can show compassion, love, care and humility. This world is not just for humans; it also belongs to all creatures. Remember that, my son, remember that."

Granddad had heard grandma's raised voice and came to see what the commotion was about, even though he knew very well what it would be about. Grandma and granddad would never agree on the treatment of animals. Neither of them wanted to cause a scene, so grandma became silent and continued with her chores and granddad smoked his pipe. The atmosphere was tense. Even Dengo Tier, Ewu the goat, Okookoo the hen and Chicken Dawn seemed to be doing their chores in silence.

By the time gran had finished cooking, cleaning and talking to granddad about the preparations for the New Yam festival, it was quite late in the afternoon. It was now peaceful and quiet but this was suddenly interrupted by the town crier. "Listen brothers and sisters," he cried. "The king has declared that the New Year celebrations can begin! Please make your way to the Palace Square for the first event, which is the blessing of the Hunting. Chidi could hear the noises of men, women and children blowing horns and beating pots and pans as they made their way to the Palace Square. Chidi had to quickly collect the eggs and feed the chickens then, he could join the hunters to capture the antelope.

Two boys Obi and Tarik Amina's brother arrived at the house. They immediately went round to the back to find Chidi grinning broadly. Obi was one of Chidi's cousins. He was a tall boy who could not talk. He was always happy. Obi smiled at Chidi and placed his hand on his chest and then on Chidi's chest as a greeting. The boys went to find Chidi's grandma and granddad. They were sitting on the front porch. Obi leaned forward to greet them.

Obi picked up a stick and began to draw a picture of an antelope in the sand. He gestured to Chidi to come to the Palace Square. Obi could feel the vibrations as men and women marched along. "Make sure you gather the eggs, change the water in the ete and bring back the firewood before you leave," instructed his grandmother. Chidi could tell by the tone of her voice that she was not happy that he was going to the hunt. But he wanted to be a man. A MAN. The antelope would make him a man.

"Yes Ma," Chidi replied as he closed the door behind him.

A part of him wanted to call the whole thing off but he couldn't. He had to be a man. It had almost become an obsession for Chidi, as he listened to the chanting of the crowds and the beating of the drums. He had made up his mind that he was going to hunt. Chidi, Tarik and Obi, together with Dengo Tier the dog, quickly completed the chores and made their way to the Palace Square. Chidi's grandfather was already there at the Palace Square. He was representing the red cap chiefs, while grandma abstained. The crowd at the Palace Square was made up of men, women, boys and a handful of girls. A man stood on a raised platform; he was dressed in a khaki shirt and shorts with a loincloth over the top. He was covered with white chalk, called nzu, which represented purity. He was the Eyese the kingmaker.

The Eyese asked everyone now to be silent, as the Eze the king was about to appear on his throne. The king made his way to his throne, walking in the traditional zigzag rather than in a straight line. He wore a decorated robe and red coral beads adorned his head. His face was decorated with nzu.

Warriors and red-capped chiefs, who wore wraps around their waists, escorted the Eze. Chidi's grandfather was among them. The women chiefs wore wraps around their chests and beads on their necks, arms and wrists. There were a number of young boys who were still in training, just like Chidi was. Although she was a chief Chidi's grandmother abstained from this part of the ceremony. She did not believe that animals should be hunted like this. The crowd blew horns and sang traditional songs. Some people began taking photographs with their phones, cameras and camcorders.

Two warriors brought out traditional spears and a large pot.

By this time the king had reached his throne. Chidi recognised him though he looked very different. He looked very formal and not too happy. Chidi remembered a king who wore a baseball cap, humbled enough to pick up plantains for a lady. He was almost unrecognisable. He was adorned with beads and totally transformed, almost like a statue. He had sited Chidi in the crowd and smiled briefly at him. Then the king stood still and gestured for everyone to be quiet. Silence fell and everyone watched him. He then began to pray and all the people bowed their heads to receive a blessing. After praying, the king threw nzu into the air and all the chiefs did the same. The white nzu landed on people's heads.

"We may now go to hunt, and we thank God for this," announced the Eyese. Unfortunately Chidi couldn't hear all of his speech. It was crowded and he wasn't tall enough to see what was going on. "Remember just one antelope is all we need to usher in the New Year," cried the Eyese from the platform.

"Just one antelope would make me a man," Chidi said to himself.
The crowd once again began to shout. Some of the women and girls began to cook so that when the hunt was over the men would have something to eat.

People began to split off into small groups. The group that Chidi, Obi Tarik and Dengo Tier joined was called 'Odinma' meaning 'it is good' and was made up of six men, ten boys, four women and two girls. They began making their way to the bush.

After a long walk the group finally arrived at the bush. They saw other groups of hunters and tracks that others had left. Some of the men and women were wearing eye protection mostly sunglasses. Others wore face protectors similar to those used by welders and builders. Chidi was puzzled by this and by some of things people were carrying. They had spears, cutlasses, sticks, lamps, torches and other various objects he was not too sure of.

After a while the ground started to become increasingly dusty. The crowd began to move faster, dragging and scuffing their feet, kicking the earth and sending dust flying into the air. It made it hard for Chidi to see where he was going, and the air smelt dusty and dry. He stopped for a while and leaned his body forward to try to catch his breath.

Chidi rubbed his eyes to clear his vision. He remembered the eye gear he had seen some people wearing and now understood why. He was being pushed and pulled around by the crowd as everyone was struggling to see where they were going. Chidi became disorientated and lost his sense of direction, so he stood still to try to regain his bearings. He knew he had been separated from his friends and from Dengo. He could taste the fine dust that had settled on his lips and it became a little difficult for him to breathe. He tried coughing but this didn't help.

Chidi sensed that he wasn't alone even though he was separated from the rest of his group. He could hear the sound of breathing nearby. The dust began to settle and he could make out a blurred shape very close to him. Suddenly his vision cleared and Chidi found himself face to face with an antelope. There was silence. Chidi could hear his heart beating louder and louder. Human and animal both stood very still, staring intently at one another, both afraid to move a muscle.

Chidi stared at the antelope. It had large horns and dark brown spots on its hind legs. Still frozen to the spot, he remembered that these animals sometimes attack humans. Very slowly he began to move away from the animal. As he was edging away, the back of his right foot struck a small rock. He stooped to pick it up and throw it at the animal, but something made him stop.

Chidi noticed that the animal was making painful grunting sounds. He looked more closely and saw that it was injured. Feeling brave, or stupid – call it what you will – he approached the antelope and saw that its front left foot was caught in a trap. Chidi no longer felt the need to end the life of this animal, rather he felt a connection with it.

The trap was sharp but Chidi decided that he must take it off. He knelt down, placed both hands in the spiky opening and began to pull the sides apart. This allowed the antelope to remove its foot. He was so intent on his task that he didn't realise that the trap was making his fingers bleed quite badly.

Chidi tore his white handkerchief into strips. It was covered in blood now anyway. He used the strips to bandage the antelope's leg. Almost as a gesture of appreciation, the antelope began licking his bleeding hands and fingers. Chidi knew his mum and dad were not going to be too pleased when they saw his shirt.

Chidi looked at the antelope. "How do you feel now? Can you stand up?" he asked gently. At that very moment he heard footsteps and the voices of hunters.

"You're in great danger. You must leave at once," Chidi said. He gestured to the antelope to get up and pointed to a path in the bush so it could run away.

In his quest to help the antelope escape, Chidi, who was walking backwards, tripped over a thick twig, fell and hit his head on a log. The antelope saw this and turned around to check on him. It sniffed at Chidi, who was lying in the floor, licked him and circled around him. It tried to wake Chidi up by licking his face, but Chidi wouldn't wake up, so the antelope decided to lie down beside the young boy who had shown him such love and care. It began to make a loud grunting noise to attract the attention of the hunters so that they would come and help Chidi.

After a while the antelope still had no success. He either had to wake Chidi up or attract the attention of the hunters. He had decided. It stood up and tried to pull Chidi with its mouth towards the hunters this proved difficult. Once again it made a loud noise to attract their attention. Chidi by now was beginning to wake up and was drifting in and out of consciousness.

The first to appear at the scene were Obi, Tarik and Dengo. They were shocked to find themselves face to face with an antelope. They didn't immediately see Chidi lying wounded on the floor.

Chidi was by now not fully awake but he did his best to gesture to the antelope to run away. But the antelope completely ignored him. Instead, it began to make even louder grunting sounds that would be sure to attract the attention of the hunters.

"Shh!" said Chidi to the antelope, and put his finger to his lips.

Chidi turned to look at Obi, Tarik and Dengo. They were still in shock, their eyes firmly fixed on the antelope. Finally, Obi turned his attention to his cousin and went to see whether he was okay. Dengo moved closer to the antelope and growled. Chidi drew a finger picture on the floor to instruct his cousin Obi to try to hide the antelope.

The antelope kept licking Chidi's face, only stopping to make the loud grunting noises. Chidi continued to plead with it to stop making so much noise. "Leave, you silly beast"! Don't you know you'll be killed? Go!"

Chidi gave the huge antelope a great big push in the direction of a nearby path. The antelope still wouldn't go, but instead pranced backwards and forwards between Chidi and the path. Its persistent grunting noises soon began to attract the attention of the other hunters and their footsteps could be heard coming closer.

Obi thought for a moment while the antelope continued to make the loud grunting sounds. The hunters eventually and certainly heard the sounds, and made their way to where it was coming from. When they arrived at the scene they were quite astonished at what they saw. Obi had thought quickly, and had begun to prance around, and miming to the grunting sounds the antelope was making. He was flapping his arms up and down and pouting to make the grunting sound. Dengo-Tier felt quite embarrassed by this human behaviour. He had frankly never really understood human beings and their strange behaviour.

Chidi heard one of the hunter's call out to him. He asked him if he had seen any antelope. Chidi didn't know what to say and still had not fully recovered from his ordeal. He however remembered that three people had given him advice about telling lies. Little did he know that this was his first test of becoming a man. He now held a life in his hands. Sitting up on the floor with the support of his friend Tarik he began to recall all the advice he received from three people. Meanwhile the hunters waited for an answer while Obi muffled the grunting sound of the antelope.

**Decision time for Chidi**
The first person who had spoken to him about lying was his mum, whose advice went like this: "Under no circumstances must you ever tell me lies." To follow that advice now would mean that the antelope would be captured and its life would be in danger.

The second piece of advice was from his teacher. This was very similar to his mother's advice: "It is better to talk things over and find a solution rather than to tell a lie." That was no good either, Chidi thought. The animal would still be killed.

The third piece of advice was from his dear beloved grandma, who often saw life in a different way to other people. She once told Chidi that he must always try to tell the truth but that he could reserve one lie for each year. This lie, however, could only be used to save a life. Chidi decided to follow the advice of his grandma, as he felt that it was the only advice that would allow the antelope a greater chance of not being captured.

Chidi got up and called out **"No."** He moved his body so that he was shielding the injured animal from being seen. Satisfied that Chidi was okay, and there was no antelope nearby, the hunters moved on.

Chidi turned to look at the antelope. It almost seemed to have tears in its eyes, as if it were saying thank you and was grateful for Chidi's help.

It took some time for the antelope to leave Chidi, even though the hunters were nearby. Obi led it to a nearby bush and carefully hid it. He had just finished as another group of hunters arrived.

"What is wrong with you, child?" the first hunter asked Obi.

"You know he can't talk," said the other hunter. "Look Chidi is hurt. That's why he's making such a noise." The hunters' attention was so focused on Chidi and getting him home as they could see he that the back of his head was bleeding. They did not notice the antelope behind the bush. "How did this happen, Chidi?" asked one of the hunters.

Chidi thought for a moment and said, "Well, you see, a big blue whale came and punched me in the belly and I fell."

"There are no whales in the bush!" said one of the hunters.

"This child is crazy; we take him to his mama," the other suggested.

The two hunters took Chidi, Obi, Tarik and Dengo Tier back to Chidi's grandma's home. As they went Chidi turned to look at the antelope that was still hiding in the bush. They said goodbye with their eyes knowing that they would always be good friends.

When the group arrived at grandma's home she was surprised to see Chidi in such a state. She cleared the long couch so Chidi could lie down and sent Obi to find a wrap so she could cover him properly. She looked quite cross although she had tears in her eyes as well. As the hunters told her what had happened, she tended to Chidi's wound, cleaning and dressing it. She stayed very silent placing her right fist under his chin. Her left hand was free to inspect the rest of his head. Her steady gaze at her grandson gave her an indication that Chidi had more to say to her. She turned to thank the hunters for bringing him home and gave Dengo, Obi and Tarik the am not pleased with you look.

Grandma saw the hunters out and thanked them again for bringing Chidi home. Then Granddad came in. Grandma looked a little cross with him but said nothing. She turned to Chidi her grandson and gave him a loving hug and said very calmly, "Thank God you're all right now start talking and leave nothing out."

Chidi began to cry softly as he told his grandmother everything that had happened. He looked at her, and said, "I'm sorry. I told more than one lie." Grandma began to think, pacing up and down the room as she always did when she was thinking. She turned to Chidi and said, "No, you did not."

## Grandma's explanation

Chidi looked at his grandma. She had that look on her face, the one she always had when she was about to share her wisdom. "Do you remember what your last homework was about, Chidi? Fractions! You see, according to the rule of fractions, you have told one whole lie to save a life, but you did it in sections, like screens in a play, or like fractions. The first part was to bandage the antelope's leg; the second part was to hide the antelope from the hunters and the third was to make up a story to save its life. That, my son, is you making a very big decision to save a life. You are truly a man."

Grandma smiled then gave Chidi a hug and told him not to worry about his mum and dad. She walked away into the kitchen. Chidi was puzzled by what his grandmother had just said. He looked at Obi, Tarik and Dengo Tier to see whether they could give him an explanation, but they just smiled.

Seeing his granddad and uncle Dubie walk into the room, Chidi wanted to say a big hello to them, but he suddenly held his throat and found himself unable to speak. He had lost his voice. He had to settle for a big hug from them instead. Grandma Comfort walked in with a big bowl of hot herbal bitter leaf soup on a tray. She placed it on a stool next to Chidi and said to him "This will help your sore throat. If you drink this soup I am very sure your voice will begin to return." Chidi sipped at the soup, it wasn't called 'bitter leaf soup' for nothing.

His mobile phone rang with a text message. Chidi looked at the message and smiled. It said,

"Hi it's me. Heard what happened to u and what you did for that antelope.
If u r not doing anything meet me at the cinema tomorrow 2pm. Bring

enough coins for popcorn. I might be able to listen to your excuse for ignoring me yesterday. Amina"

Chidi sent a reply: "I will be there."

It was amazing what a text message could do for a sore throat. In just one minute Chidi had gulped down the soup, leaving everyone speechless.

Chidi's phone rang with another message. If it were even possible, this was better than Amina's text. It was from his dad: "Just to let you know that your mum and sister have been summoned by grandma Comfort to stay with her for a couple of days. They are on their way now. "Your room is safe. Love, Dad."

Chidi had nothing left to worry about. He only had to decide what to wear for his big date at the cinema. Little did he know that trouble was brewing at the palace. The text read **HELP. EZE.**